ROSIE'S DREAM CAPE

Rosie's Dream Cape

ZELDA FREEDMAN

Illustrations by
Silvana Bevilacqua

RONSDALE PRESS

ROSIE'S DREAM CAPE

RONSDALE PRESS
3350 West 21st Avenue
Vancouver, B.C., Canada V6S 1G7
www.ronsdalepress.com

Typesetting: Julie Cochrane, in Minion 12 pt on 16
Cover Art: Silvana Bevilacqua
Cover Design: Julie Cochrane
Paper: Ancient Forest Friendly Rolland "Enviro" — 100% post-consumer waste, totally chlorine-free and acid-free

Ronsdale Press wishes to thank the Canada Council for the Arts, the Government of Canada through the Book Publishing Industry Development Program (BPIDP), and the Province of British Columbia through the British Columbia Arts Council for their support of its publishing program.

Library and Archives Canada Cataloguing in Publication
Freedman, Zelda
Rosie's dream cape / Zelda Freedman.

ISBN 1-55380-025-7

1. Child labor — Ontario — Toronto — Juvenile fiction. 2. Immigrants — Ontario — Toronto — Juvenile fiction. I. Title.

PS8611.R43R68 2005 jC813'.6 C2005-900260-3

At Ronsdale Press we are committed to protecting the environment. To this end we are working with Markets Initiative (www.oldgrowthfree.com) and printers to phase out our use of paper produced from ancient forests. This book is one step towards that goal.

Printed in Canada by AGMV Marquis

For Momma and Poppa,
my family and friends

MY PROMISE

My Momma, Rosie Swedlove an immigrant from Odessa, Russia, came to Toronto, Canada, in January 1921. She was eleven years old when she started working in Yitzy's "sweat-shop" factory.

It was called a sweatshop because the girls, and in some factories, even boys, were forced to work during the hot sticky summer in smelly crowded rooms with no windows or air conditioning.

There are still sweatshops today in many cities all over the world. Some are in secret places where it is hard to find them. And very young children still slave over their sewing machines just as Momma did.

Momma sewed coats and capes for the fancy ladies on the rich side of town.

When she was very old and sick, Momma told me for the first time about some of her experiences in that factory.

She made me promise to tell her story to you.

And I have kept my promise.

Zelda Freedman
Ottawa, Canada

Chapter One

"Faster," growled Yitzy, the boss of the sweatshop. "Quit wasting time, and don't steal the scraps. They aren't your business." He slammed his fist on Rosie's sewing table. "In my factory you follow my rules. You understand?"

Rosie's eyes were glued to her sewing machine. "I understand," she said softly.

Her hands trembled. She squinted and pulled the red thread through the hole in the needle. Her heart thumped. She rubbed the dark circles under her eyes. She tossed her long, frizzy braid over her shoulder. She looked younger than eleven.

She wiggled her frail body to the edge of the wooden bench and stretched her skinny right leg out to the black metal foot pedal on the floor.

Rosie leaned forward. She slowly slid the red velvet cape towards her until the needle was on top of the pocket. She pumped the pedal slowly. The needle bobbed up and down in a steady rhythm. Then she pumped faster and faster, making straight, even stitches.

The only light came from a dirty bulb that dangled above her head.

Yitzy leaned down until his face was level with Rosie's. She felt his breath on her cheeks.

He glared at her. His beady eyes bulged out of his head.

Rosie stopped pumping. She looked up.

"You," he said, shaking his grubby fingers at her, "you listen to me carefully. You make sure you hear me. I tell you once, I tell you a million times. You watch out for those inspectors. You can tell when they're coming. You'll hear their footsteps on the stairs. Their heavy boots go clunk, clunk. You hear what I say?" he said, rubbing the jiggling, black mole on his chin.

"Ye . . . yes," said Rosie, her voice shaking.

"If you hear the inspectors coming, you run and hide in the toilet. The law's the law. Remember this. You're supposed to be fourteen to work here. Don't make trouble for me. You understand? And don't steal the scraps, they aren't your business."

"I understand."

Yitzy leaned on Rosie's table. His fat belly hung over the side. "You wanna know something else? Those inspectors, they could close me down. They'd finish me off."

He slid his hand across his neck as if to slit his throat. "*Kaput*, finished. Got it?"

"Ye . . . yes," said Rosie.

The year was 1921. Rosie Swedlove, a Jewish immigrant from Odessa, Russia, had come to Toronto with her grandmother Bubba Sarah. They lived in a three-room apartment above Mr. Yacobovitch's flower shop, at the corner of Dundas and Spadina streets, right where the streetcar stopped.

Since her arrival in Toronto in January nine months earlier, Rosie had been working at Yitzy's garment factory. She had sewn evening coats, spring coats and raincoats for the fancy ladies on the rich side of town. Fancy ladies. That's what Yitzy called them.

Rosie earned five dollars a week. And with the money Bubba Sarah made from sewing alterations at home for the neighbours, they were able to make ends meet.

"Don't worry," said Bubba Sarah. "We'll be just fine."

But Rosie knew that they couldn't survive without her pay.

Rosie worked from early morning until seven o'clock at night every day except Sunday. That was her special day. Only Bubba and Mr. Yacobovitch knew what Rosie did on Sunday.

Every Sunday at exactly twelve noon, since Rosie had arrived in Toronto, she climbed into the streetcar at the corner of Dundas and Spadina, dropped her five cents in the slot, and sat in the seat right behind the driver. The streetcar went along Spadina Avenue, to King Street West.

"Next stop, King Street West," the driver would call out.

Rosie would jump up, smile at the driver, hop off the streetcar, and skip along the street to the Royal Alexandra Theatre.

Chapter Two

Yitzy's factory was on Spadina Avenue, just before Adelaide Street West, and about eight blocks from where Rosie lived. It was on the top floor of the red brick Morris building. The four flights of rickety wooden stairs up to the factory shook like an earthquake when all the sewing machines were working.

Sixteen girls worked in the one-room factory. The room was large with green walls, a peeling plaster ceiling and badly marked wooden floorboards.

There were four long tables in rows with three or four girls at each table. They sat on wooden folding chairs that would creak whenever the girls stood up or sat back down.

Some girls sat hunched over their tables for most of the day measuring and cutting the velvet and the linings. Others basted, making huge stitches and sewing the backs and fronts of the capes together. The girls who ironed sat at narrow ironing tables on high stools. Several older girls sat at one table carefully stitching the edges of the linings, the pockets and the collars.

At one end of the room, opposite the entrance, was Yitzy's office. His door was usually kept shut but there was a grimy glass-paned window looking out onto the factory floor. Sometimes the girls would see him standing by the window, watching them work. Shelves on his office walls were piled high to the ceiling with bolts of wool, gabardine, heavy silks, linings and velvet. Narrow shelves stored threads, ribbons, buttons and patterns. Yitzy was careful to lock the door to his office whenever he left the factory.

There was a lunch table beside the bathroom, but the factory had a damp musty smell from the steam of the irons and many of the girls chose to eat their meals sitting on the wooden steps outside the factory door.

Rosie was a "finisher." She sat by herself at a long table that was placed near Yitzy's office window so he could keep an eye on her. Beside Rosie's table was a clothes rack where she hung the capes once they were finished. Only sewers with steady hands were finishers. Each stitch had to be straight, even, not too tight, but not too loose.

"To be a finisher you gotta make perfect stitches," said Yitzy. "There is no room for mistakes." He slid his hands through his greasy black hair. "You ruin the material, you pay. And then I'll have to order lots of extra material, and you'll have to do the job over again. You got it? You understand?" he said.

"Ye . . . yes," said Rosie.

Rosie hated it when Yitzy stared at her. His eyes reminded her of the Cossacks, those bad soldiers, and that horrible night with her mother. She cringed at the memory.

Rosie slipped her hand into the deep pocket of her brown and green checkered apron that Bubba Sarah had sewn from the leftover kitchen curtain scraps. She clutched the little red and black flowered change purse, holding it tightly and prayed that the older girls, mean Fenya and fat Gitel, wouldn't notice.

"You should leave your purse at home," said Bubba Sarah. "You listen to what I tell you. It's no good to be stubborn."

But Rosie wanted her purse in her apron pocket. "I really need it," sighed Rosie. "I just feel better when I can touch it."

"If you're not careful, someone will take it. I warn you," said Bubba Sarah.

"I'll be careful, you'll see," said Rosie.

Momma had given Rosie the purse.

And to think that she had almost forgotten it on that night when she and Bubba Sarah had fled Russia for Canada.

"Here," Momma had said, "a little souvenir to remember this night when I danced in the Swan Lake ballet at the opera house in Odessa." Momma had kissed Rosie on the forehead. "There are eighteen kopecks — pennies — in here. They are for good luck. In Hebrew, eighteen is the word *chai,* which means 'to life.' Keep this purse always for good luck."

Some luck, thought Rosie. How could all this have happened? Poppa had died when Rosie was seven. Too young to die, Momma had said. Then Bubba Sarah came to live with Momma and Rosie. Bubba Sarah designed and sewed all of Momma's clothes. Only the latest styles for your Momma, Bubba Sarah had said.

After Poppa died, Momma had made so many promises. She had promised Rosie ballet lessons. And she had promised that Bubba Sarah would sew Rosie a cape just like her own.

But none of that would ever happen now.

"Listen here, everybody," shouted Yitzy as he banged his fist on Rosie's table. "Today we begin sewing the velvet capes for Christmas. This season Eaton's ordered six dozen capes — two dozen black and four dozen red. So, you got the rest of October to finish the two dozen black capes, and the whole month of November to sew four dozen red capes, some with pink trim and some all red. Remember what I told you about velvet. You gotta be extra careful not to ruin the material. Yah, you understand?"

"Yes," they said.

Yitzy carefully piled pieces of velvet on the cutting tables.

At the end of each table were huge bins on rollers which held lining material and other supplies.

"You see these capes," said Yitzy, pointing to the pile at the end of Rosie's sewing table. "Only Eaton's Department Store sells a Yitzy cape," he bragged, sticking out his chest. "This year I got the biggest order yet. Six dozen capes for the holidays! Remember you got till the end of November to finish them all. So quit fooling around, and don't steal the scraps. You hear, November not December," he shouted. "And don't make trouble."

Rosie shivered as the howling wind swirled through the cracks in the broken window next to her table. People said it would be an early winter. It was only October and already it was cold. She squirmed in her seat. She sat on her hands to warm them.

But nothing could keep her warm, not even the yellow sweater that Bubba Sarah had knit — the one with the uneven shoulders, and the too-long sleeves. And certainly not the cotton flannel purple skirt that was two sizes too big.

Rosie knew there was no use complaining.

"Better the skirt should be too big than too small," said Bubba Sarah. But then Bubba Sarah said that about all of Rosie's clothes.

"Don't worry, you'll grow into these clothes."

But Rosie did worry.

Rosie worried about many things. She couldn't talk to Bubba Sarah like she had talked to Momma. Bubba Sarah was seventy-five years old. How could she understand?

Rosie never told Bubba Sarah that she always ate her lunch alone at her sewing table or that every day Fenya pulled her braid and whispered mean things about her. She never told her about the shooting pains in her neck from bending over the machine or about the cramps in her legs from stretching to reach the foot pedal or how her eyes stung from squinting because of the poor light and how, on some days, her fingers were so cold she couldn't thread the needle.

Chapter Three

One morning in late October, while piling the capes on Rosie's table, Yitzy said, "Listen here, you wanna make an extra dollar a week? All you gotta do is sweep up the scraps at the end of the day. Pile them into these empty sugar bags, and put the bags in the cupboard beside the steps. Yah?"

"Okay," said Rosie.

"Then at the end of the week, I'll take the bags down to the street for the garbage. You understand?"

"Yes," she said, "I understand." But Rosie didn't really understand. Why would Yitzy throw out such beautiful red and pink and black velvet scraps?

Every morning Rosie arrived at the factory half an hour early hoping to avoid Fenya and Gitel's teasing.

Inside her bench, Rosie kept her apron, folded neatly at the end of her shift, her tin containing her sewing tools, and her lunch of a banana, two pieces of rye bread and butter, a cinnamon roll, and a jar of juice. Also stored in the bench was the suit pattern from the *Woman's Home Companion*, which Rosie had found near some empty boxes on the stairs. One day, she thought, I'll sew a suit like that.

She took out her apron, pulled it over her head, tied a bow in the back, emptied the tin can, and neatly placed all her sewing tools on her table. She was proud of her sewing tools. Bubba Sarah had given them to her.

"Here," Bubba Sarah said, "these tools, they come from Odessa. They will do you for all of your life." And she placed them into the empty baking soda tin.

Rosie loved the metal thimble best. It was a half size, and

didn't cover the finger tip. It was different from other thimbles. You couldn't buy one like that at the Morris building. This one fit perfectly on her small finger.

Behind Rosie, at a long narrow table, sitting on high stools were Fenya and Gitel. They were "pressers." They ironed all day long. The hot steam gushed in their faces, and smeared the rouge plastered all over their cheeks.

"Hey Yitzy," called out Fenya. "How come Miss Rosie gets to be a 'finisher?' Me and Gitel, we've been here four years and all we get to do is iron. You call that fair?"

"Fair, schmair," shouted Yitzy. "You don't like it, then leave. You understand?"

"Yah," piped in Fenya, pulling down her too tight sweater. "I understand. Right, Gitel?" she said, poking Gitel in the ribs.

"Yah, you're right, Fenya," said Gitel, nodding. She wore her hair piled high on her head.

"And another thing," said Fenya, "you think it's fun to lift these heavy, hot irons all day? And *she's* just a newcomer," she said, pointing to Rosie.

Then she stuck out her tongue. "And anyway, what could a little immigrant girl know? Aren't I right, Gitel?"

"Yah, you're always right," said Gitel, her fat hips drooping over her stool.

"And just look at Miss Rosie," said Fenya, pointing to Rosie's apron. "See that ugly apron. It's gotta be made from dumb scraps. Scraps! Who'd ever save scraps?"

"You Fenya, listen here," said Yitzy. "Mind your business, and don't nobody steal my scraps."

"That's all you ever say, Yitzy. A million times a day. Don't steal the scraps," mimicked Fenya. "Don't steal the scraps."

"Right," piped in Gitel, scratching the pimples on her forehead.

"And another thing," said Fenya. "Tell me, Miss Rosie, what do you do on Sundays? I'll bet all you do is sit at home and twiddle your thumbs. Anyway, where would a puny girl like you go? Not like us, eh Gitel?"

"Sure," said Gitel, rolling her eyes. She was afraid to tell Fenya the truth. She never did anything on Sunday.

"Like I care what any of you do on Sunday," said Yitzy. "You don't like it here Fenya, too bad. There are lots of big, strong girls out there who can hold a heavy iron. Pressers are a dime a dozen. You understand?"

"So, how come *she* gets a dollar more for sweeping up the scraps?" demanded Fenya.

"Huh . . . like you Fenya, you'd stay late to sweep up the scraps? Who you kidding, eh? Not you. You're too lazy. You'll never be a finisher, not in my factory. You got clumsy, ugly hands, you got a big mouth, and you talk too much. You think I don't hear or see what goes on?"

"I don't got ugly hands," said Fenya, pointing to Rosie. "She's the ugly one."

Then Fenya yanked Rosie's braid and sang:

"Rosie, Rosie, you're so small,
You'll never amount to anything at all,
With an apron like that, and nothin' to show
You'll never go anywhere important yah know."

And she burst out laughing.

And at home Rosie cried to Bubba Sarah, "Fenya and Gitel, they laugh at me."

"Forget about them," said Bubba Sarah, "but you better listen to me, and bring your purse home. It's not safe there."

Bubba Sarah was probably right about the purse.

Rosie took it home. She counted the eighteen pennies, and then carefully placed her little red and black flowered purse under her pillow. "I know it'll always be safe here."

Bubba Sarah smiled. She straightened her black kerchief on her head, and tied it in a knot at the back of her neck. A few strands of white hair hung over her forehead.

Rosie hugged Bubba Sarah and nestled her head against her grandmother's shoulder. That skirt and blouse, how I hate them, thought Rosie. They had that musty smell, just like the smell on the boat. If only Bubba Sarah would throw those clothes out, thought Rosie. But not Bubba Sarah, she saved everything.

How could Rosie forget those days on the boat? Rosie had snuggled close to Bubba Sarah in that bunk bed. The boat rocked back and forth.

Bubba Sarah used her skirt as a blanket to keep Rosie warm.

And the dormitory room, in the basement of the boat, stank from people being sick. Everybody was huddled together like animals. They called it steerage class. You call that "class," Bubba Sarah had said, to sleep in a room with no windows?

And after two weeks at sea, Rosie and Bubba Sarah landed in Halifax and soon after, boarded a train to Toronto and their new life in Canada.

Chapter Four

Rosie hated Fenya. She hated her more then anybody in the whole world. She hated Gitel too. But some days she wasn't sure whether to hate Gitel or feel sorry for her.

Rosie placed a cape under the needle. From a pile on her table, she picked up a red velvet piece that was a pocket. She closed her eyes and gently rubbed the soft cloth against her cheek. It was smooth and silky and felt just like Momma's velvet cape. She shook her head, smoothed out her green and brown checked apron, bent forward, and placed the velvet under the needle.

Some days Rosie worked until ten o'clock at night. Then she carefully folded her apron, and placed it neatly inside her bench. She opened the baking soda tin can, the one that Bubba Sarah had saved, the one with the pretty lady painted on it, and she put her thimble, and needles and small embroidery scissors in it. Then she closed the bench.

She wrapped her brown scarf three times around her neck, put on her gray and black tweed coat, pulled down her purple hat to cover her ears, slipped on her black lace-up boots, and ran home.

The sky was black, the street was empty, and the bitter wind blew in her face.

How could all this have happened? Her life in Odessa was perfect, she thought. She had friends. She had everything she needed. She didn't come from a poor family but she wasn't a princess in a castle either. And here she was stuck working in a factory. It just wasn't fair.

Every day Yitzy piled a bunch of capes at the end of Rosie's table. "Your quota for today," he said. "That's the number of capes I put here in this pile. You gotta finish all of them by the end of the day. You understand?"

"Yes," said Rosie.

And if you get behind," said Yitzy, "you'll have to come back and work on Sunday. You hear me?"

"Ye . . . yes," said Rosie. But there was no way Rosie was ever going to work on Sunday. Sunday was the day she went to the Royal Alexandra Theatre. She had never missed a Sunday since she came to Toronto. She was just happy to stand at the railing beside the big carved wooden doors and watch the people go in, and dream that maybe one day she would be able to go in too. Being there reminded her of those days when she went to the theatre to watch Momma dance in the ballet. She remembered how they walked hand in hand to the opera house, and Rosie wore her furry white rabbit coat with the matching hat, and her hands were warm and cozy in her white muff. And she remembered Momma wearing her black velvet cape. Bubba Sarah had designed and sewn it. There were wide flares at the bottom, and it hung down to her ankles. And it had a shiny red lining with a pattern on it, brocade material Bubba Sarah had said, and it had a big sparkling button at the neck. And when Momma walked, the cape rustled in the wind.

Chapter Five

All day long Yitzy paced back and forth, between rows and rows of tables, bumping into the girls' chairs and stools as he moved along. He inspected sleeves and collars and checked seams and linings. He watched as the girls cut out the patterns on the cutting table.

"Make sure you cut exactly to the pattern. If you cut too much, you'll pay me for the velvet you waste. Understand?"

At the end of each day, Yitzy always came back to Rosie's table. He shoved his face into hers. "You finished your quota?" he asked.

Rosie looked up. "Yes."

Yitzy pulled his horn-rimmed glasses from his pocket. Then he took out his magnifying glass and held it over the stitches. He carefully stuck his needle — first in one stitch, and then another.

"Good, good," he said, "not too tight, and not too loose. Those rich ladies, they're very fussy. You should see them. They check everything, even the stitches on the inside. So, all the stitches, they gotta be perfect. One crooked stitch, and they complain," said Yitzy. "Just keep going, and remember what I tell you, don't steal the scraps."

Yitzy never smiled.

But all Rosie could see was his black mole jiggling on his chin, and a red vein bulging from his neck. And his eyes. They frightened Rosie. They reminded her of the eyes of the Cossacks, the bad soldiers. A shiver crept up her back like a snake.

How could she ever forget what those soldiers did on that horrible night? They waited in covered trucks behind the opera house at the stage door until the ballet was over. It was rumoured that they had shoved all the dancers into the trucks and sped away firing their guns into the air, laughing and shouting.

And Momma and all the other dancers disappeared.

That night, Rosie and Bubba Sarah waited for Momma. They waited and watched until two in the morning. But Momma never came home.

Bubba Sarah had said that they took Momma for no reason. "Since when is being an artist a crime?" asked Bubba Sarah, shaking her head.

Momma was a ballerina, and she sometimes spoke out about artists' rights.

"Maybe it would have been better if she had kept quiet," said Bubba Sarah, shrugging her shoulders. "Who knows about those things? Was that an excuse to take her away? Those Cossacks, they hate peasants and gypsies, and writers and dancers. But most of all they hated Jews."

Each morning for two weeks after Momma disappeared, Rosie dragged herself to the opera, sat on the top step, and prayed that Momma would come back. She cried and cried. Her eyes became red and swollen.

Every afternoon she went to the train station hoping that Momma would appear. Rosie watched as trains arrived from Moscow and Kiev, and Leningrad and Minsk. And she watched as each person got off the train. But she never saw Momma.

Then one cold, wet, foggy night, at three in the morning, Bubba Sarah woke Rosie. "My child, my child," Bubba Sarah had said. There was such fear in her voice. "It's becoming very dangerous for us Jews to stay here. Your mother and I had saved some money in case there was trouble. The journey will be difficult but we must go. We have no choice. We must leave now. Quick, gather only enough things that will fit in this bag. And I'll fill up my metal trunk, the one with the handle on the end so we can pull it."

Rosie scrambled to collect a few things together. Then she put her arms around Bubba Sarah and wept.

"What about my friends?" cried Rosie.

"No time to say goodbye," said Bubba Sarah, as she hobbled around the apartment, stuffing the trunk. They slipped quietly down the stairs to the street.

"Oh Bubba Sarah," whispered Rosie. "I forgot the little red and black change purse that Momma gave me."

"Go quick, my child, get it, but hurry," said Bubba Sarah.

Rosie dashed back up the stairs, grabbed her purse, and shoved it into her coat pocket. She took one last look at her home and then closed the door.

Chapter Six

Rosie worried about Bubba Sarah.

Bubba Sarah had crooked legs from a streetcar accident when she was a girl. One leg was shorter than the other. She wore a shoe that had a built-up piece inside to help her walk. But she still needed a cane. Bubba Sarah tried to hide the pain, but you could see it all over her face. She hardly ever went out.

"It's the stairs," she said. "It's too hard to climb the stairs. You Rosie, you'll be my legs." Bubba Sarah always used these funny English expressions. "You'll shop and take care of things in the outside world."

And that's what Rosie did. She was Bubba Sarah's legs.

Bubba Sarah's face was full of wrinkles. Every single day she wore her black blouse and long black skirt. Her apron was sewn from the same curtain material as Rosie's.

"Please, Bubba Sarah," pleaded Rosie. "Throw out that horrible black skirt."

"Me, throw out a good skirt?" said Bubba Sarah. "Look here, it's still good. See, no rips, no holes. You give me a good reason to throw it out."

Bubba Sarah never went out. Her shoulders heaved up and down when she walked. She had pain in her legs. "The worst is the stairs," she said. And on very damp days, she needed Rosie to help her get out of bed. She knew a little English but she spoke to Rosie mostly in Yiddish.

Bubba Sarah was born in Odessa, Russia, and lived there all her life. As a girl she had sewed in a large factory with a hundred other girls. After she was married, Bubba Sarah and her husband had opened a small shop where they sold the suits and hats that she designed and sewed. Years later, when Bubba Sarah was alone, she closed the shop and moved in with Rosie's family.

Now here in Toronto, Bubba Sarah paid two dollars a month to rent a sewing machine that she kept at one end of the wooden kitchen table. She sewed for the neighbors. "A cuff here, a hem there," she said. "I make some money for us this way. It all helps."

Bubba Sarah kept her sewing supplies in the metal trunk that was pushed under the only window in the apartment. She altered Mr. Yacobovitch's clothes, his wife's clothes, and their children's clothes too, all for free. In exchange, Bubba Sarah paid less rent.

"It's a good deal for both of us," said Bubba Sarah.

And Mr. Yacobovitch agreed.

Sometimes Bubba Sarah got a big order to sew a wedding dress.

On Sunday mornings, Rosie shopped, and cleaned, and ironed, and washed the floors. Sometimes Bubba Sarah would say, "Go Rosie, go to the Morris building. I need more supplies. Buy me two yards of black cotton material, three spools number six thread in green and black, two packages of white buttons — you know the kind for a man's shirt — and a half-yard of brown corduroy material to patch Mr. Greenberg's pants."

Rosie loved the Morris building. Everybody went there. It had three floors of rooms with sewing supplies. There was a room filled with buttons: square buttons, round buttons, brass buttons, mother-of-pearl buttons, long scissors, crooked scissors, tiny scissors for embroidery, and all sizes of needles.

Another room had ribbons: red, blue and yellow ribbons, checkered ribbons, and ribbons with teeny flowers on them, and threads in shimmering gold and silver, rickrack and a million shades of black ribbons — brown-black and green-black and blue-black and jet-black.

"Oh Bubba Sarah," said Rosie, "you'd love the Morris building."

The biggest room in the Morris building had shelves from ceiling to floor with heavy rolls of green silk, velvet in red, black, pink and purple, cotton in blue and yellow, checkered materials in red and orange, and lace from Italy. Another room had stacks of patterns, and dozens of *Woman's Home Companion* magazines. One could see the latest fashions, right from New York City, and order any pattern.

On Sunday mornings when Rosie had finished her chores, she climbed on top of the trunk and watched the people hurrying up the street. There were fancy ladies rushing into Mr. Yacobovitch's flower shop, girls throwing marbles against a brick wall, boys playing hockey and the ice-man carrying huge blocks of ice. Most of the ice-men just dumped the ice outside the doors right on the street. Bubba Sarah was lucky because her ice-man always carried the block of ice into the apartment and put it into the ice box for her.

"Here," said Bubba Sarah to the ice man, "a couple of hot rolls for such a cold day." Bubba Sarah was famous for her rolls.

And Rosie would run down to the street to meet Yankel the fruit and vegetable peddler who sold his wares from the back of his truck.

""Yankel has the freshest fruit of all," said Bubba Sarah.

There was so much to see in Kensington market.

Everyone called it the Jewish People's Market. It was several blocks long. Saturdays and Sundays were the biggest market days. Lined along the sidewalk were pushcarts in front of the kosher butcher shop, the bakery, the fishmonger, the cheese shop and the dairy. Some carts were filled with dry beans, lima beans, navy beans, black peas and green peas. There were carts filled with nuts. Others had eggplants and turnips. Some pushcarts had dresses and shawls hanging from a rope like a clothesline. And all day, you could hear the peddlers shouting, "Fresh fish for sale, carp, trout, and white fish. Fresh fish for sale."

Chapter Seven

Every morning after the doors opened, Yitzy stood in front of Fenya and Gitel's table shouting, "No talking, you hear, and don't think you can steal the scraps."

"Who'd ever wanna steal those ugly scraps?" said Fenya.

"Yah," said Gitel, "who'd ever want those?"

"Not your business," said Yitzy.

Then Yitzy boasted about the big order from Eaton's. "Only the best sewers are finishers," he said. "You, Rosie, who showed you how to sew?"

"My grandmother, Bubba Sarah."

Rosie was proud. Bubba Sarah had said to her, "Your job Rosie, it's the best one in Yitzy's factory. You finish the outside edges of the capes with fancy ribbons or braid. You hand-embroider designs on the pockets and collars. And sometimes you embroider a name on the inside pocket for a special order. You're lucky."

"I know," said Rosie.

"You have golden hands," said Bubba Sarah. "And thanks-to-God, in Yitzy's factory there is no piecework. You don't ever have to do piecework. Piecework, where sometimes you work at home and you only get paid for each piece you finish. I spent years on piecework. You gotta work fast, fast. The boss, he gives you piles of collars one day, cuffs, sleeves, pockets, whatever he needs. And sometimes you sew all night, no time to sleep, no time to eat. It breaks your back. Piecework, never piecework for me again."

Bubba Sarah saved everything.

"A zipper here, a pocket there, old shirt buttons. Who knows when they might come in handy?" she said.

On Sunday morning Rosie did the laundry and scrubbed the floors. Bubba Sarah gave her a grocery list. It was scribbled in Yiddish. "Don't forget. You buy rice, and a chicken from Shlomo's Kosher butcher — from another place it might not be fresh — and a five pound bag of Five Roses Flour, and one pound of yeast for my sweet rolls, and eggs, and sour cream and nuts. You better hurry. You don't want to miss the twelve-o'clock streetcar."

An hour later Rosie emptied the straw basket filled with groceries. And at quarter to twelve she pulled on her boots. Then she took her little red and black purse from under her pillow, and slipped it into the pocket of her coat.

"Your coat," said Bubba Sarah. "Button up your coat."

That coat. Rosie couldn't even tell what colour it was. It looked like black tweed but it was all faded. The cuffs and collar had ragged edges. But it had those very deep pockets. Rosie knew her purse would be safe.

Bubba Sarah pulled Rosie's wool hat down over her ears.

"It's a bitter cold day, maybe a storm is coming," said Bubba Sarah. She twisted the scarf three times around Rosie's neck.

"I gotta hurry," said Rosie. "The streetcar, it's never late. I need to be at the Royal Alexandra Theatre at least an hour before the ballet starts. Rosie took one look in the full-length mirror. Nothing matched. Not the scarf, or the hat, or the coat or the green mitts. She closed her eyes tight and made an ugly face.

"Listen here," said Bubba Sarah sternly. "You remember Mrs. Shinder, the lady from the Jewish Immigrant Aid Society, JIAS, who met us at the train station here in Toronto. You remember that cold day?"

"Sure I remember that day," said Rosie with a sigh.

"Look what JIAS did for us. Look at this apartment. It is comfortable," said Bubba Sarah, pointing to the sturdy kitchen table, the small sofa and bureau. "They even paid our rent for our first few months here."

"I know," said Rosie impatiently. "I gotta go, Bubba Sarah. I'm getting hot."

"Yah, I know you have to go. But you listen to me," said Bubba Sarah. She had the habit of going on and on about things.

Rosie stood on one foot and then the other.

Bubba Sarah sat down in the wicker rocking chair. "So what if the wallpaper is a little faded and the chairs are crooked. We have a big oven and a warm bed and enough food to eat. We are lucky to be here in Toronto. Look at what happened to. . . . " Bubba Sarah stopped speaking as she looked up at a photo of Rosie's mother hanging on the wall.

"It's okay, Bubba Sarah," said Rosie. "I understand."

"Only God knows where we would be without JIAS," continued Bubba Sarah softly. "And just like JIAS helps the Jewish people, the Christian churches help their people. It's a good country, Canada. If I sew, and you sew, we don't need help. So you tell me, Rosie, what more could anybody want? Eh, you tell me."

"You're right Bubba Sarah, I wasn't really complaining," said Rosie. "It's just that I hate these clothes."

"So you hate those clothes. There are more important things to worry about," said Bubba Sarah, closing her eyes. Rosie looked up quickly at the clock that sat on top of the ice-box.

"It's five minutes to twelve," sang out Rosie. "I'll miss the streetcar. Bye!" She dashed down the back stairs, raced out of Mr. Yacobovitch's flower shop, and got to the corner just as the streetcar pulled up.

Rosie climbed up the steps of the streetcar, dropped her five cents into the pay box, and sat in her favourite seat behind the driver. She pressed her face against the window and stared out as the streetcar clattered along Spadina Avenue. She couldn't wait to get to the Royal Alexandra Theatre.

Twenty minutes later, the driver called out, "Anybody for King Street West?"

Rosie jumped up, and stood waiting for the bus door to open. She skipped along the few blocks and finally reached the theatre. She ran to her spot beside the tall, wooden carved doors. She leaned against the railing under the roof with all the lights shimmering in the sunlight. She slipped her hand into her pocket and squeezed her little purse. She didn't even feel the wind on her back.

Two ushers wearing black uniforms and white gloves opened the doors. They nodded and smiled at Rosie. They rolled out a red carpet all the way to the curb.

Rosie peeked inside the theatre, at the giant chandelier with the million lights, and the huge circular staircase that was covered in a royal blue carpet.

Ladies with high-heeled shoes and long flowing coats, gentlemen with top hats, boys in short pants with socks to their knees, and girls with bright bows in their hair and black shiny shoes, stepped out of the limousines and onto the red carpet, laughing and holding hands, excited to be going to the ballet.

Maybe someday, thought Rosie, I'll come to the ballet and wear a velvet cape.

Soon everyone had arrived at the theatre and the ushers closed the giant doors. Rosie happily ran up the street to wait for the streetcar, and headed for home. It was another perfect Sunday, she thought.

Chapter Eight

One evening while Rosie was sweeping up the scraps, she studied the large red and pink pieces of velvet lying on the floor. Sometimes Yitzy used the pink pieces for trim and other times he used red rickrack. Suddenly Rosie had an idea. A cape, she thought, a beautiful cape from all these pieces. Me and Bubba Sarah, we could sew a wonderful cape. Rosie's heart beat faster and faster. She bit her lip. She hesitated. She stroked the red scraps. It was the best colour of all. Should I or shouldn't I? Her eyes darted around the room. She took a deep breath, grabbed the scraps and stuffed them into her pockets. Rosie felt funny doing this without permission. But it wasn't *really* stealing. Yitzy never used these scraps. And anyway, every Friday afternoon she saw him drag a bag of scraps out to the street

Rosie sweeping up the scraps

for the garbagemen. What difference would it make if she were to take a few pieces of velvet? Yitzy would never miss them. Rosie decided there was no reason to worry. Bubba Sarah was right. A good sewer should save the scraps, and big pockets in the ugly apron did come in handy.

And at home, for the next few weeks, Rosie emptied her pockets of many scraps of all sizes. Bubba Sarah was happy to help Rosie sew the pieces together. They attached the red pieces by hand embroidering strips of pink velvet all around the red velvet. And the cape got bigger and bigger.

"It's nice of Yitzy to give you these scraps," said Bubba Sarah. "Now all we need are two big pieces of material, one for the hood, another one for the collar. And two small ones for the pockets. So beautiful," she said, holding it up to the light. "*Vunderbar,* wonderful."

Rosie squirmed in her chair. She looked down at the floor. How could she tell Bubba Sarah the truth? There were many things she didn't tell Bubba Sarah.

Bubba Sarah smoothed out the material. "It's nearly finished," she said. "I'm happy for you, Rosie, but you really belong in school. A young girl like you shouldn't be breaking your back in a factory. It made Bubba Sarah very sad to think that Rosie had to work. "It seems only immigrant children don't have to go to school," she added thoughtfully. "Let's hope maybe someday things will change."

Rosie understood what Bubba Sarah meant.

Rosie and Bubba Sarah celebrated the Sabbath at home

every Friday night, by saying prayers over Bubba Sarah's candlesticks. Bubba Sarah kept all the traditions for the holidays. She cooked matzah ball soup for Passover, and baked a round challah, egg bread with raisins in it, for the New Year. Bubba Sarah would have liked to go to the synagogue but it was too far away for her to walk there.

One evening, while Rosie and Bubba Sarah were working on the cape, Rosie asked, "Bubba Sarah, why does Yitzy tell us not to steal the scraps, then he takes them down to the street for the garbage?"

"Who knows?" said Bubba Sarah. "It's not your problem."

"I guess," said Rosie. "And another thing. I hate the way Yitzy hangs around my table more than anybody else's. He yells at me, do this, finish that. Then he piles up more capes. And he keeps saying over and over again, 'You understand?' He always picks on me. Why?"

"Because you are a 'finisher,' Rosie. It's a very important job," said Bubba Sarah. "The most important job in the shop."

"I suppose," mumbled Rosie. Her heart beat faster. She was so ashamed of what she had done. She wondered if this cape was such a good idea after all.

Chapter Nine

Another Sunday came.

At ten to twelve, Rosie bolted down the back stairs and ran through Mr. Yacobovitch's flower shop.

"Pick up your flowers on the way home," called Mr. Yacobovitch.

"Okay," called Rosie, "see you later."

Such a nice man, thought Rosie, just like Poppa.

At twelve o'clock sharp, the streetcar stopped at the corner. Rosie climbed in. Soon she was at the Royal Alexandra Theatre.

While Rosie waited for the limousines to arrive, she thought about many things. She thought about how terrible she was for stealing the scraps, and what she was going to do about that, and she thought about what she had told her Momma. "Some day, Momma," she had said, "you'll see. I'm gonna sew nice clothes and design them myself." And Momma used to shake her head and say, "My Rosie, ever since she was little, she had fancy ideas. She was born wearing beautiful clothes."

She slipped her hand in her pocket and squeezed her red and black purse. And she thought about how when visitors came to her house in Odessa, if she didn't think she looked nice, she wouldn't come out of her room. But all that was so long ago.

Soon a shiny black car drove up. They called it a Rolls Royce. A funny name for a car, thought Rosie.

A lady stepped out.

Rosie couldn't believe what she saw. The lady wore a black velvet cape, and it had a collar that stood up and black braid on the pockets. The cape looked just like one that Rosie had sewn in Yitzy's factory.

Then a girl, about six years old, jumped out. She was wearing a purple coat with white fur around the collar and cuffs. A little boy followed. He bent down to pull up his navy socks that had fallen beneath his knees. The children laughed excitedly and ran into the theatre.

Once everyone was inside, the ushers rolled up the carpet and closed the doors.

Rosie headed home. It was cold, and a gentle snow started to fall.

Rosie ran through Mr. Yacobovitch's shop.

"A good time?" he asked. "Here, your flowers." He handed Rosie a bunch of red roses, yellow daffodils, blue forget-me-nots and purple irises. "I can't sell flowers that are drooping," he said. "Tomorrow, Monday, I get fresh ones. You and Bubba Sarah, enjoy. And thank your grandmother for those hot cinnamon rolls with the sticky bottom. I could smell them baking from here," he said, smacking his lips.

Bubba Sarah stood waiting at the top of the stairs for Rosie. She held out a plate full of sweet rolls. Rosie gobbled two down even before she took off her coat.

"Guess what I saw, Bubba Sarah?" said Rosie, her face flushed with excitement. "There was this lady wearing a cape just like the ones from Yitzy's factory. And it had black braid on it. Do you think it was one that I sewed?"

"It could happen."

"Oh Bubba Sarah," said Rosie. "I am lucky. Sunday is the very best day of all."

"If you say so," said Bubba Sarah.

Chapter Ten

The next day, after work, while Rosie was sweeping up the scraps, she spied two large pieces of red velvet on the floor. They were just what she needed for her cape. She glanced around nervously. Yitzy had left to run an errand. No one was around.

Suddenly, the door burst open, and Fenya stumbled in just as Rosie was stuffing the scrap pieces into her apron pocket.

Rosie gasped. She didn't know where to look. She pulled her hand out of her pocket but it was too late. The scraps fell to the floor. She stared at Fenya.

"Hah, caught you stealing, eh?" said Fenya, smirking. "Miss Rosie, sneaking around and stealing. You think you're so smart." She put her hands on her hips and stuck out her chest. "I left my purse on my chair, or did you take that too?"

Rosie stood still. She was too frightened to speak.

"Wait till I tell Yitzy," sneered Fenya. "Boy, you're in trouble now. You'll get fired. And you'll never work again. First, you'll see, the inspectors will come. Then they'll call the police and they'll put you in jail. That's where you belong. And after you rot in jail, they'll send you back to Russia. And who knows what the police will do to Yitzy. So what do yah think of that?"

Fenya picked up her purse and dashed out the door. "Just wait until tomorrow," she called.

And Rosie could hear her shout as she ran down the stairs:

> *"Rosie, little thief, and oh so small*
> *where you'll be going won't be a ball."*

Rosie couldn't stop shaking. Goose bumps covered her body. They felt like bugs crawling all over her. Her face was hot and sweaty. Her knees shook. She threw her apron down, and left her needles, thimble and scissors out on the table.

She grabbed her coat, fled down the stairs and ran out to the street.

"What will happen to me?" she cried. Tears streamed down her cheeks. Fenya was right, she thought, they'll put me in jail. Maybe I won't go home. Maybe I'll vanish, just like Momma did.

Rosie was glad that Mr. Yacobovitch was busy with a customer so she didn't have to talk to him. She dragged herself up the stairs into the apartment and plopped down at the kitchen table.

Bubba Sarah took one look at her. "You must be sick. Look, your eyes, so red, and your cheeks, burning." She put her hand on Rosie's forehead. "You got a fever?"

"I, um, I don't feel good," mumbled Rosie.

"A little chicken soup?" asked Bubba Sarah.

"No, I just wanna go to bed."

Bubba Sarah tucked her into bed.

For a long time Rosie lay still, just staring at the ceiling. She put her hand under her pillow and clutched her red and black purse. Then she buried her head in her pillow and cried herself to sleep.

Early next morning Rosie shoved her dream cape into the dresser drawer in her bedroom.

Bubba Sarah hobbled into the kitchen. "Maybe you don't go to work today. Here, some tea and honey."

"No Bubba, I gotta go to work. I gotta finish my quota or Yitzy will be mad."

Rosie didn't have the courage to tell Bubba Sarah the truth. She sipped her tea slowly.

Rosie walked down the stairs and out to the street. She poked her way along the sidewalk kicking stones with her boot. What will I do if Yitzy fires me? she thought. I need money for rent. Maybe I could sell Bubba Sarah's home-made jars of jams, and peaches, and pickles. Other people set up stands at the Kensington market and they sell things. But how could she ask Bubba Sarah to do that?

Rosie dragged herself up the stairs to the factory.

Chapter Eleven

"Listen here, Rosie," said Yitzy. "How come you're late today? And why did you leave your apron on the floor last night?" He gave her a mean look as he stacked a pile of collars and pockets at the end of Rosie's table.

Rosie pulled her apron over her head. Nothing mattered anymore.

"So Rosie," said Yitzy. "Today you sew these pockets and collars on the capes. Okay?" Rosie's hands shook as she tried once, then twice, to thread the needle of the sewing machine. Her head pounded. She knew she would never amount to anything. How could she do such a terrible thing?

Fenya leaned over to Gitel. "Guess what?" She pretended to whisper, but she talked loud enough so that Rosie could hear. "Last night, I saw Miss Rosie stealing the scraps." She poked Rosie in the back. "You know, Gitel, those big ugly scraps."

Gitel gasped. "Oh my God, are you sure? Is that true?"

"Yah, yah, I'm sure," said Fenya. "I saw it with my own eyes. So Gitel, what do you think about that?"

Gitel kept her head down as she slowly moved the iron back and forth over the material.

"So, when do you think I should tell Yitzy?"

"I don't know," said Gitel.

"Now? Today? Or make Rosie suffer a little? What d'yah think?"

Gitel said nothing.

"What's the matter with you?"

Gitel looked up.

There stood Yitzy, his hands on his hips.

"You, Fenya," he grumbled. "Quit your talking." He shook his finger at her. "And listen everybody in here," he shouted. "Get to work, and don't think you can steal the scraps."

Fenya doubled up, roaring with laughter. "Now ain't that the funniest thing I ever heard."

Gitel kept her eyes on her iron.

For the rest of the day, whenever Fenya had a chance, she pulled Rosie's braid. "Poor, poor Miss Rosie. Just wait till I tell Yitzy."

"Why are you so mean to Rosie?" asked Gitel. It was the first time Gitel had talked back to Fenya.

"Because I could do a better job sewing than Rosie, and

I could be the best finisher in this place if I wanted to be. So there," she snapped. "And another thing, Yitzy doesn't call *her* ugly and stupid. As if I really care. She thinks she's *so* smart. And anyway, I don't have to give *you* a reason. She's a thief, not a finisher, that's what she is."

"'You know what, Fenya?" said Gitel. "I think you're jealous of Rosie. That's what I think."

"Are you crazy?" said Fenya. "Me, jealous of HER. That's the funniest thing I ever heard."

Later that day Yitzy stacked more pockets and collars on Rosie's table. He peered through his magnifying glass to check her stitches.

"Look at this work," he grumbled as he held up one pocket to the light. "See, this one's got holes in it." Rosie cringed. She couldn't stop her hands from shaking.

Yitzy rubbed the mole on his chin. "You know velvet is delicate. You can't rip stitches. You can only make an embroidery stitch once and that's that. You can't sew over it. I told you before. You ruin the material, I charge you. That's the rules. This time I keep some of your pay, plain and simple."

Rosie's stomach felt like a barrel had rolled over it. Her arms hung down her sides like lead.

All day Fenya had threatened to tell. But she didn't tell Yitzy that day, or the next day, or the one after that.

Chapter Twelve

At home, Bubba Sarah asked, "You feeling better, Rosie?"

"So-so," she would answer.

But for Rosie, every day was worse than the one before. She wanted to die. There would be no more job, no velvet cape, no more Sundays at the Royal Alexandra Theatre. Nothing.

Bubba Sarah tried to make Rosie feel better. "Here, some soup. It'll make you feel better." She smiled and kissed Rosie on the forehead. "Maybe tonight we work on your cape. We didn't work on it for a few days. And it's nearly finished."

Bubba Sarah went to the bedroom and opened the drawer. "What's this?" she said, very surprised. "It's all creased. You didn't fold it properly." The cape was squished up in a ball. "Your cape, you threw it in the drawer? After all our hard work. What's the matter with you?"

Rosie burst into tears

Bubba Sarah stood there holding the cape up against her black skirt. "Like a piece of junk it looks."

Rosie burst into tears.

"Oh Bubba Sarah," cried Rosie. "I did a terrible thing. I stole those scraps. Yitzy never gave them to me."

"You what? You did what?" Bubba Sarah shouted. She shouted so loud that even Mr. Yacobovitch probably heard her.

"I . . . um, I stole the scraps for my cape."

"And here I am, helping you," said Bubba Sarah. "And every day I said to myself, what a nice boss Mr. Yitzy is. I thought he gave you the scraps." She shook her head so hard, her kerchief fell off. "I'm ashamed. Why? Why you do this? You fooled me. My Rosie is a thief? Stealing. For what? A shame for me, and a shame for the neighbors. Your mother would turn in her grave."

Rosie had never heard Bubba Sarah sound so angry.

"I didn't mean it. I really didn't mean to steal," sobbed Rosie. "I just wanted to have a velvet cape like Momma's, like the one she promised me. I know Yitzy told us not to steal the scraps. But he never used them. He just threw them in the garbage."

Rosie wiped her nose on her sleeve. "I'm sorry, Bubba Sarah. I'm really sorry." She tried to hug Bubba Sarah. She didn't even mind the horrible, musty smell from Bubba Sarah's blouse and skirt.

Bubba Sarah didn't hug her back. She pushed Rosie away.

And she kept saying over and over again, "Imagine, my Rosie stealing."

Rosie sank into the chair. She buried her head in her arms. "There's something else," she said, wiping her eyes. "Fenya saw me taking the scraps, and she said she'd tell Yitzy, and I would be fired, and the police will put me in jail and then they'll send me back to Russia." The faster Rosie talked the more she cried.

Bubba Sarah wasn't even listening. She limped around the kitchen table, clutching the cape. "My Rosie, stealing. I can't believe it. It's a blessing your Momma isn't alive to see this. From where you get such a crazy idea?"

"It started when I saw those big pieces of red velvet lying on the floor," said Rosie. "And since Yitzy never used them, I figured it didn't matter, and he wouldn't miss them," she sobbed. "Why does he make such a fuss about the scraps? Why does he act that way?"

"It's not how he acts that counts, but how YOU act," Bubba Sarah said, catching her breath. "But I want to tell you something. Long ago when I was a girl, I also worked in a sewing factory. Many days the boss announced, don't take the material from the floor. I need to count every piece, he said. Just leave everything on the floor. In those days who would question a boss? Never. Even a piece of thread we wouldn't take. Years later I found out why."

"Why?" asked Rosie rubbing her eyes.

"You see, the boss, he figured if he frightened us, we

wouldn't steal a new piece of material, or some buttons, or maybe some spools of thread, or a zipper. Who knows what else? But that doesn't mean it's okay for you to steal."

"I wasn't stealing important things," said Rosie.

"Stealing is stealing," said Bubba Sarah. She banged her hand on the table so hard that Rosie jumped.

"A thief is a thief," said Bubba Sarah. "Tomorrow morning, first thing, you take this cape back. Phooey, poison, that's what this cape is. I never want to see it again." Bubba Sarah folded the cape and shoved it into a brown paper bag. "You hear what I say?"

"Ye . . . yes, I hear you."

Chapter Thirteen

It rained the next morning. Rosie walked slowly along the wet street. In the brown bag under her arm, pressed close to her side, was her dream cape.

It usually took Rosie about twenty minutes to walk to the factory but today it took her longer. She was late. She climbed the four flights of stairs. She tiptoed to her table, and placed the paper bag on the floor next to the foot pedal.

"What's going on around here?" said Yitzy. "How come you're late, Rosie?"

"I dunno," she said, as she stared at the floor.

"And where's Fenya?" he asked. "Yah I know, she's late again. I'm gonna take some money off her paycheck. That should smarten her up." He walked over to the door to wait for Fenya.

Gitel was busy ironing. She gently tapped Rosie on the shoulder. "Rosie," she said with a shy smile. "Tell Yitzy. You gotta tell him. He's not that bad. I know 'cause I've been here a long time. He acts like a lion but he's really a pussy-cat. I've seen lots of things happen here. He isn't really mean. He just acts that way. Tell him yourself before Fenya tells him. It's better this way. Honest it is."

It was the first time Gitel had said something to Rosie, as if she really cared.

Fenya pranced into the room a few minutes later. She was surprised to see Yitzy waiting for her.

"Listen here," he said. "Every day you're the last one in and the first one out. I've had enough with you. You'll get less pay this week. Understand?"

Fenya stuck out her chest. "Huh" she said. She walked to her table and sat down on her stool.

"So," said Fenya, jabbing Rosie in the back, "today's the day. Yah, today's the day. Right, Gitel?"

Gitel didn't answer.

Rosie kept her head down, and threaded the needle of the sewing machine.

Yitzy came by with a bunch of capes. He stacked them, one by one, at the end of Rosie's table. "These, they gotta be done today. You stay till they're done, no matter how late? You understand?"

Rosie looked up, bit her lip, and burst into tears.

"What's the matter with you today?" asked Yitzy.

"I, um, I stole some scraps," Rosie blurted out. "Red ones and some pink ones. I didn't mean to steal. I thought you didn't need them. I'm sorry. It was wrong. I shouldn't have done it."

Fenya stood up and put her hands on her hips.

"Well," she said. "I might be late, but at least I'm not a thief like Rosie. I knew she was a thief a long time ago. Gitel knew that too."

Gitel sat rigid on her stool listening carefully.

Yitzy stared at Rosie. His eyes opened wide. He shook his head. "You what? You stole? In my factory? Doesn't anybody around here ever listen? How many times did I tell you not to steal the scraps? You understand English or not?"

"Ye . . . yes," said Rosie, wiping the tears from her eyes. Rosie's heart banged louder than the clanging machines.

"You got the scraps with you?" asked Yitzy.

"Here," said Rosie, bending down to pick up the paper bag. "They're in here." She struggled to open the bag. Her fingers trembled.

Yitzy grabbed the bag from Rosie, turned it upside down and shook it. "What's this?" he shouted, as the cape fell onto the table. "You, you made a cape?"

"Ye . . . yes."

"But I told you, a thousand times, don't steal the scraps." Yitzy was furious. And then out of habit, he bent down and stuck his needle in a few stitches. He rubbed his hand over the creases. "Huh," he said out loud. "Who do you think you are, stealing my scraps?" Then he grabbed the cape and stomped away.

Gitel tapped Rosie on the shoulder. "You'll be okay," she said in a gentle voice.

"Don't count on it," said Fenya, sarcastically. Rosie bent her head over her sewing machine. She wondered if Yitzy was going to fire her.

A moment later he was back, standing by her table. "So, Rosie, you make big trouble for me. You proud of what you did?"

"No," said Rosie in a whisper.

"It's a bad time of year," he mumbled. "You had to make trouble for me, eh? I gotta deliver these capes to Eaton's Department store on time. So, how do you think I'm gonna do that? Yah, I know I got other sewers, but no other good finishers, and anyway the girl who starts a cape should be the same one that finishes it. It's the only way. Then the stitches are all the same. This order, it can't be late." He paced back and forth in front of Rosie's table, rubbing his mole and repeating, "You tell me, what am I gonna do now?"

Rosie looked up. The dark circles beneath her eyes were wet with tears. There was nothing she could say.

"Okay," said Yitzy, pointing his finger in front of her face. "Here's what I do. I punish you this way. You continue to work until the Eaton's order is finished. You work every day late. You work Sunday. You get no pay. After the order is finished I'll decide what else to do to you. You still sweep the scraps. That's your job. You understand?"

Rosie nodded.

"First it's Fenya and then it's Rosie," said Yitzy. He marched off to his office and slammed the door. A few minutes later he opened the door and shouted, "I'm going outside. Everybody in here get to work."

He always went outside to smoke a cigar when he was angry.

Chapter Fourteen

While Yitzy shouted at Rosie, Fenya had been nodding her head looking pleased. “So there, Miss Rosie,” she said, yanking Rosie’s braid. “Serves you right. You’ll work with no pay, work Saturdays and Sundays, work late every night. Hah. I’ll bet you’ll soon be gone from here, gone forever, and that suits me just fine.”

Then Fenya poked Gitel. “So,” she said, “what do you think of that?”

“I’ll tell you what I think,” said Gitel, her hands folded across her chest. “I think that Rosie’s cape is prettier than the ones we make here. *That’s* what I think.”

Fenya picked up her stool, banged it on the floor, and sat with her back to Gitel. “I’m finished with you,” she said. “You know it’s a stupid, ugly cape, made from those dumb scraps. You call that cape pretty? I wouldn't be caught dead wearing it."

"Well, that's your opinion," said Gitel, her hands on her hips.

Then Gitel turned to Rosie. "Hey Rosie, you wanna have lunch with me today?"

It would be the first time that Rosie didn't have to eat her lunch alone.

After that, Rosie trusted Gitel. She told her everything. She told her how she and Bubba Sarah had worked on the cape every night, and that she called it her dream cape. She told her about Momma and the ballet, and the red and black purse, and where she went on Sunday, and about wishing she had enough money to buy a ticket to go to the theatre.

Rosie worked late for many nights. Her eyes were red and stinging from the poor light. And on Sunday she worked until ten o'clock in the evening. At home she climbed on top of the trunk and stared out the window. Her life was ruined.

Bubba Sarah didn't talk much.

Rosie couldn't look Bubba Sarah in the eye.

Even Mr. Yacobovitch noticed something was wrong. "How come you don't smile anymore?" he asked. "And you work Sunday. Why?"

Rosie vowed never to tell a soul. She was a thief, as bad as those pickpockets on the street. And when the Eaton's job was finished, there would be no job, no money, no dream cape, nothing.

On the last Sunday in November, Rosie arrived early for work. Besides Yitzy, she was the only person in the factory. A dozen capes were piled high on her table. The pockets and collars had to be attached, and the braid had to be sewn on the outside seams.

"This is the week," said Yitzy. "No fooling around. Just this pile left."

"Don't worry, Yitzy," said Rosie. "I'll finish them, I promise I will."

"Fine, fine," said Yitzy. "If you need something, I'm in my office. Just knock." He closed the door behind him and pulled down the blind over his office window. He always pulled down the blind when he was working on his bills.

Rosie took a cape from the top of the pile. She placed a strip of red braid on the collar. She held the cape tight as she moved it under the needle. Then she pulled the cape with one hand, and flattened the braid firmly with her other hand. She pumped the pedal, slowly at first, then faster and faster.

Bubba Sarah had said that sewing braid was the hardest job of all. With braid you had to think of nothing but the stitches. You look up, you make a mistake.

At first Rosie's machine hummed quietly. She kept her head low, watching every stitch. The faster she pumped, the louder the noise.

Suddenly Rosie heard a funny noise. Thump, thump. The thumps became louder and louder.

Rosie stopped pumping. She pulled the cape tight to her chest. Her heart sank. She dared not look up. Her blood turned to ice. In front of her, all she could see were two pairs of heavy, black boots. Slowly she looked up. Two men, one tall and the other bald, stood in front of her.

They took their badges out of their vest pockets and held them up for Rosie to see.

"You know who we are?" said the bald man. "We're factory inspectors. What's your name? How come you're working on Sunday?"

Rosie tried to speak but her tongue felt numb.

"You, girl," said the tall inspector. He had a hoarse voice. "You got a name?"

Rosie wanted to run and hide but it was too late.

The tall inspector slid his hand through his hair. He pulled his glasses off his hooked nose and looked around the room.

"You got papers?" growled the bald inspector. His loud voice echoed in the empty room.

Rosie looked straight ahead. The floor and ceiling were spinning around her.

The tall inspector yanked a pad from his jacket pocket. He began writing. "You lose your tongue? You going to talk or not?"

"Yes sir." Rosie swallowed hard.

"You got a name?"

"My name is Rosie Swedlove, sir."

"So, you going to tell me how old you are?"

"Yes sir. I, um, I'm fourteen."

"Sure don't look it to me. You got papers to prove it?" asked the bald inspector.

"I . . . um, I forgot them at home," mumbled Rosie.

"How long have you been in this country? You're supposed to carry your papers with you. You don't remember the immigration officer telling you that?"

"Ye . . . yes sir, I remember. But I, uh, I just forgot them." Rosie choked on her words.

"Where's your boss?" asked the bald inspector.

Rosie pointed to Yitzy's office. "There," she said.

The inspectors marched across the room and banged on Yitzy's door.

Yitzy opened the door. His mouth dropped and his eyes opened wide. "Since when you inspect on Sunday?" he asked scratching the mole on his chin.

"Why not?" snapped the fat inspector. "And we'll be back again to see if that girl's got papers." He pointed to Rosie. "She sure looks young to me."

"No problem," said Yitzy smiling, "she's got papers."

"Caught you off guard, eh?" said the tall inspector, smirking.

"No, not at all," said Yitzy in a calm voice. He pretended nothing was wrong. He held out his hand. "Come in, come in," he said smiling.

Rosie had never heard Yitzy talk so nice like that before.

"We talk. Okay?" said Yitzy. He put his arm on the tall inspector's shoulder and motioned both men into his office. Yitzy gave Rosie a hard look before closing the door.

Chapter Fifteen

Rosie tore off her apron. She grabbed her coat, raced down the stairs and ran as fast as she could all the way home.

"Bubba Sarah," she cried, bursting through the door and choking on her tears. "The inspectors, they came. I didn't have time to hide. They asked me my name and how old I was. They wanted to see my papers, and they said they'd be back again to see my papers, and when they went into Yitzy's office I ran away. Oh Bubba Sarah, what's gonna happen to me? Will they put me in jail?"

"It's all right, my child," said Bubba Sarah calmly. She kissed Rosie on the forehead. "No, they won't put you in jail. Somehow we'll fix the problem. Don't worry." But Bubba Sarah was worried and her stomach was in knots. "Rosie, Rosie, what am I going to do with you?" she said. "It's always something. First you steal and then you get in trouble with the inspectors."

"I hate it here in Toronto," cried Rosie. "We should never have come here. I wish I could go back to Odessa." Rosie's whole body shook.

"Nonsense. You know that's not possible," said Bubba Sarah. "Our life is here. We have to make the best of it."

For the rest of the day, Rosie sat on the trunk, crying.

"What will happen to Yitzy's factory, and that order from Eaton's? What will happen to you and me, Bubba Sarah? It's all my fault. If I had heard the inspectors on the steps, I could have hidden in the toilet like Yitzy warned me to do." Rosie sobbed. It was too awful to think about. "I have to think of some way to fix this."

That night Rosie woke up screaming so loud that Bubba Sarah nearly fell out of bed.

"Oh Bubba Sarah, I had this horrible dream. Bad soldiers came and put handcuffs on me, and dangled my red and black flowered change purse in front of my eyes, and then left me outside in the cold." Rosie slipped her hand under her pillow to make sure her purse was still there.

Rosie couldn't stop shivering.

Bubba Sarah hugged her tightly. "Go back to sleep, we'll talk in the morning."

Rosie wondered how she could finish the capes. If only she could think of something. She fell back asleep, still clutching her Momma's change purse.

Early the next morning, Rosie woke Bubba Sarah up.

"Oh Bubba Sarah," she said, tugging at Bubba Sarah's nightgown. "I have an idea. Maybe we could go and talk to Yitzy. We could explain to him that we will do piecework at home, and that we can finish the capes on time. There won't be time at the factory and the inspectors might come back."

"Me, doing piecework? I don't do piecework no more. It's too hard, all day, all night, bent over the machine. I'm too old," said Bubba Sarah.

"I know you said you'd never do piecework again, but maybe just one more time? Please, oh please, Bubba Sarah," begged Rosie. "I can do most of the work and you can help me, a stitch here, a button there. I'll stay up all night. We still have five days left. It's only Monday. Please, Bubba Sarah, come with me to Yitzy's factory."

"What can I say?" said Bubba Sarah, shaking her head. "Me, walk on the bumpy sidewalk. How is that possible?"

"We'll take our time. We'll walk real slow. We can sit on the bench at the corner. You can rest. I know it's hard for you. But this way Yitzy can keep his promise to Eaton's."

Bubba Sarah shook her head. "Do I have a choice?" she said. "Well, maybe together we can do it. For you, I'll try."

Rosie and Bubba Sarah bundled up in their warm coats and scarves.

Rosie held Bubba Sarah's arm tightly as they headed down the stairs, one step at a time.

"I need to rest a little," said Bubba Sarah.

"Well, well," said Mr. Yacobovitch, smiling at the two of them. "How nice to see you, Bubba Sarah. What's the occasion?"

"Just business," said Bubba Sarah. "Serious business."

They finally reached the corner. They crossed the street.

Bubba Sarah hobbled past Joe's fish market, Schlomo's kosher butcher shop, Yankel the fruit and vegetable peddler, and the pushcarts filled with pots and pans and all sorts of wares.

In front of Mendele's bakery was a bench.

"I need to catch my breath," said Bubba Sarah.

Rosie and Bubba Sarah sat on the bench and rested.

Bubba Sarah recognized Mrs. Bookman and Mrs. Sobcuff coming out of the bakery. She had altered some of their clothes.

"How nice to see you out, Mrs. Swedlove," said Mrs. Sobcuff.

Bubba Sarah nodded. "Nice to see you too."

"You know, Rosie," said Bubba Sarah, "it's good to go out. Thank you. Maybe I come out more often."

Rosie slipped her arm around Bubba Sarah's arm and leaned close to her as they walked slowly up the street. The air was brisk and the sun shone brightly, and Bubba Sarah didn't even mind the cold.

"Bubba Sarah, I'll be happy to take you out anytime," said Rosie, beaming from ear to ear. "One more block and we'll be there."

Chapter Sixteen

At the factory, Rosie saw Yitzy standing outside smoking a cigar.

"There's Yitzy," said Rosie. "When he's worried he goes outside and smokes a cigar."

Yitzy spotted Rosie. He put his hands in his pocket, straightened his back, and rubbed the mole on his chin. He said nothing. He just stared at her.

"Good morning, Mr. Yitzy," said Bubba Sarah. She held out her hand.

Yitzy kept his hands in his pockets.

"This is my grandmother, Mrs. Swedlove," said Rosie.

"What you doing here, Rosie?" he asked in an angry voice.

"Me and my grandmother, we need to talk to you. I'm

really sorry for what happened," said Rosie. "I didn't have time to hide because the machine was so loud I didn't hear the inspectors come in."

"Yah, yah, I know, I know," said Yitzy. "You left me stuck with a dozen capes." He shook his head. "Big trouble. That's all I get from you, Rosie."

He turned to Bubba Sarah. "Those capes, they were to be ready for this Saturday," he said in Yiddish. "You tell me, what I'm going to tell Eaton's? You tell me, hah?"

"Eaton's, don't worry about Eaton's, they'll get their capes," said Bubba Sarah. "We have a plan. We will finish your capes at our apartment. This way we don't need to worry whether the inspectors will come. We'll sew the braid and the buttons, we'll embroider the pockets, whatever you need. You can pick up the finished goods on Friday night. You'll have your order for Eaton's on Saturday, just like you promised. I think it's a good plan. What do you think?"

Yitzy shifted from one foot to the other. He hemmed and he hawed. He looked up at the sky, and down at the sidewalk.

"You sure?" he grumbled, rubbing his mole.

"When I give my word, I give my word," said Bubba Sarah.

"Fine," he said, "I'll bring you the capes this afternoon."

"We live above Mr. Yacobovitch's flower shop, at the corner of Dundas and Spadina," said Rosie. She smiled hopefully at Yitzy but he turned and walked into the factory without saying another word.

"Don't worry, Rosie," said Bubba Sarah. "Yitzy will bring the capes. He needs you to help him finish this order for Eaton's."

Bubba Sarah was right. Later that afternoon, Yitzy delivered a dozen capes as well as the braid, embroidery thread, buttons, pockets, and linings — everything they needed to finish the capes.

"I'll be back Friday night," Yitzy growled as he left the apartment.

Bubba Sarah and Rosie worked that afternoon, that night, and all the next day and night. They took turns sleeping, a few hours here, and a few hours there. By Friday evening the capes were ready.

"It's true, Bubba Sarah, piecework is hard," said Rosie as she rubbed her eyes, and stretched her weary arms. On the table in front of her lay the pile of finished capes, each one perfectly sewn and finished by her and Bubba Sarah.

There was a knock at the door. Bubba Sarah got up too quickly, and she grabbed her back to stop the pain. She hobbled slowly to the door. "Piecework is not for me," she groaned.

"Good evening, Mister Yitzy. The capes, they're ready. Come in."

Yitzy brought in a stack of cardboard coat boxes. He spread out a huge white cloth. Then he laid each cape down on the floor. He inspected every one. He checked the stitches, snooped in the pockets and examined the lining.

"Good, very good," he said. He smiled the biggest smile Rosie had ever seen. "And the braid," he said, "it lies flat. Those fancy ladies on the rich side of town, they're gonna like these capes. This was a big year for red." He held one up in front of the long mirror. "Nice," he said, "really nice." Rosie and Bubba Sarah smiled at each other.

Yitzy gently wrapped each cape in white tissue paper. He placed one on top of the other in the cardboard boxes. "It's a good job you did. Me, I'm satisfied. Eaton's will get the rest of the order just like I promised. But let me tell you, for a while I was pretty worried."

"I'm sorry I made so much trouble," said Rosie.

"Sorry, schmorry, forget it. You wanna work again?"

"But the inspectors," said Rosie, "they wanted my papers. They said they would come back. They know my name."

"Aich, those inspectors, I know their tricks. The other day when they came, I gave them each a bottle of whisky, some expensive cigars and a little money on the side. Then we talked about life and they got quiet. Once a year the inspectors come. I try to keep them happy. It doesn't always work. For now, I don't worry until next year. But since they didn't come back this week, I'm pretty sure they won't come again until next year. They don't have time to keep coming around to the same place twice. So, what do you think? You wanna come back? On Monday we start the evening coats for spring. I got nice green and blue silk, heavy silk from Europe."

"Yes, I'll come," said Rosie grinning from ear to ear.

"Okay," said Yitzy, "tomorrow is Saturday. You come in the morning, early. I just wanna show you the new patterns, and the silk material. It's a good idea for you to practise a little on the sewing machine before we start the serious business on Monday. You know silk, it's a very slippery and delicate material. It's hard to handle. Okay?"

"Yes," said Rosie, "I'll be there."

Yitzy tied up the boxes. "Thank you, Rosie, and thank you, Mrs. Swedlove," he said, and quickly left.

"Well, Rosie," said Bubba Sarah, "our plan worked." She heaved a sigh of relief.

Rosie smothered Bubba Sarah with kisses and hugged her tightly.

Bubba Sarah sank into her chair, and fell fast asleep.

Chapter Seventeen

Early Saturday morning Rosie dashed out the door, raced down the stairs, ran through Mr. Yacobovitch's shop and out into the street. Maybe Toronto wasn't so bad after all.

At the factory, Rosie took the stairs two at a time. She opened her bench and pulled out her apron. Someone had folded it ever so neatly. She quickly put it on. She looked in the bench for the little can with her embroidery needles, her thimble and her scissors. But they were gone. Rosie's face crumpled and tears welled up in her eyes.

Yitzy walked into the room.

"What's the matter this time?" he asked

"It's my sewing tools, the ones Bubba Sarah gave me. They're gone. Somebody took them."

"Don't worry, Rosie," said Yitzy. "On Monday morning, I'll ask the girls about it. Maybe Fenya or Gitel put it somewhere by mistake when you were gone. Meanwhile I'll lend you some tools. Here is the new coat pattern for spring. And here are some small green and blue pieces of silk that you can practise with. But before you start, come to my office. I wanna show you something."

Yitzy put his arm around Rosie. "I don't know how to say this." His voice was soft, and his eyes didn't bulge out of his head. "If somebody steals scraps in my factory, it's my job to do something about it. You know, a boss, he's gotta do what he's gotta do. What can I tell you? For years I tell the girls not to steal the scraps. It's a habit for me. You know, we all do things for different reasons, and I got my reasons. That's my style."

"I understand," said Rosie. Bubba Sarah was probably right about bosses scaring the workers so they wouldn't steal.

"Okay," said Yitzy. "That's enough about stealing the scraps. I believe you have learned your lesson. Here, I got something I wanna show you." He opened his cupboard and took out the brown paper bag.

Rosie's eyes opened wide.

Yitzy pulled out her cape. He laid it down on his desk and rubbed out the creases.

"This cape, it needs a good ironing," he said. Then he pulled out from his back pocket two extra large pieces of red velvet. "One for the collar and one for the hood. Here's some extra pink pieces for the edges, and two square pieces for the pockets." He stood back, admiring the cape. Rosie was speechless.

"You know," said Yitzy, "it's really a beautiful cape, even nicer than the ones we make here. I like how you sewed the pink pieces around the edges of the red velvet. Very smart."

Rosie's eyes filled with tears. She had forgotten how beautiful the cape was.

"I gotta tell you," said Yitzy, "you have to thank Gitel. She came to see me last Monday. She's a good girl, not like Fenya. She asked me if I still had the cape. 'Yah, yah, I still got it,' I told her. Gitel said she found some red velvet scraps, big enough to finish your cape. She asked me if she could save them for you. And I said, 'why not?'"

Rosie stared up at Yitzy. She could not believe this was the same man she had been frightened of for so long. He was not like the Cossacks at all.

"So," he said in a gentle voice, "take these pieces home and finish the job. If you don't got enough material, you come back. I'll give you more." Yitzy coughed nervously and cleared his throat. "Gitel tells me you go to the Royal Alexandra Theatre every Sunday, and you stand outside watching the people arrive, and that in Odessa you went to the ballet all the time to see your mother dance."

"Yes," said Rosie. "It's true, that's what I do every Sunday."

"She also said you got a dream to go to the ballet and wear a beautiful cape. And you want to design clothes?"

"Uh huh." Rosie nodded.

"And she said you got a little change purse that your Momma gave you for good luck. So, who knows, maybe here in Toronto your dreams could come true. Now go, that's all I got to say."

Yitzy wasn't comfortable with small talk. He handed Rosie the brown paper bag. "Here, take it." He patted her on the shoulder. "Go already. Go practise with the silk. You'll see it's very slippery. You have to make sure you keep it flat under the needle," he said. "You know, Rosie, you're a very good worker."

Chapter Eighteen

Rosie couldn't wait to tell Bubba Sarah. She ran into the apartment, clutching the paper bag to her chest.

"Look, Bubba Sarah," she shrieked. "I got my cape back. Yitzy saved my cape. Come see. Quick." She pulled the cape out of the bag and spread it over the kitchen table. "And you know what Gitel did? She asked Yitzy if she could save some big scraps for me so I could finish the hood and the collar and the pockets, and here they are." She held them up in the air. "And you know what else Gitel did? She told Yitzy everything about me, and about Momma, and the ballet at the Royal Alexandra Theatre, and what I do on Sundays, and about my dream cape. And guess what, Bubba Sarah? Yitzy told me that if I needed more material to finish the cape, he would give me whatever I wanted."

Rosie's eyes sparkled.

Bubba Sarah smiled. She had not seen Rosie so happy in months.

Bubba Sarah and Rosie finished the cape that evening.

"It's beautiful," cried Rosie. She carefully lifted the cape over her shoulders and pulled the hood over her head. She stood in front of the mirror, turning to the right, and turning to the left, and curtsying just like a ballerina.

"You see, Rosie," said Bubba Sarah, "you do have good luck after all."

Later that night, after Rosie had fallen asleep, Bubba Sarah opened the trunk. She pulled out from the bottom, a piece of red brocade, heavy silk.

"The best material for a lining," she whispered to herself.

Bubba Sarah sewed the lining into Rosie's cape. Then she sewed on a big sparkling button at the neck.

She spread out a white sheet on the floor beside Rosie's bed and laid the cape down with the sparkling button on top. She folded the cape so that the red lining showed.

Rosie awoke early Sunday morning. She was excited to be going back to the Royal Alexandra Theatre. She rolled over on her side and looked down at the floor beside her bed. There was her cape, more beautiful than ever. Was she still dreaming? Rosie jumped out of bed.

"The lining, the lining," she shouted. "And the sparkling button, Momma's sparkling button. Where did they come from?"

"Well, it's like this," said Bubba Sarah, picking off short red threads from her black skirt. "That night when I packed before we left Odessa, I found a piece of red brocade, left over from the lining of your Momma's cape. So I said to myself, maybe someday I could use it. And when I went through your Momma's clothes, I knew I couldn't take her cape, so I decided to cut off the button. I thought who knows what I can use it for. It couldn't hurt to take it."

Rosie rubbed the lining on her cheek, and kissed the sparkling button. She danced around the room, pointing her toe this way and that. At last she had her dream cape. Then she carefully placed it down on the sheet beside her bed, just the way Bubba Sarah had done.

"Today, Rosie, forget about the groceries," said Bubba Sarah. "Just wash the floor and do the ironing. You'll get the groceries another time."

It was funny how Bubba Sarah understood exactly how Rosie felt.

Chapter Nineteen

"I gotta hurry," murmured Rosie. "I don't want to be late for the twelve o'clock streetcar."

"Look outside," said Bubba Sarah. "So much snow. They were right when they said we would have snow very early this year." She bundled Rosie's scarf around her neck, and pulled her hat over her forehead.

Rosie grabbed her coat, slipped her red and black change purse into her pocket, pulled on her boots and hugged Bubba Sarah goodbye.

Soon Rosie was at the Royal Alexandra Theatre, standing beside the wooden carved doors, waiting, and watching and dreaming. She didn't even notice the heavy flakes of snow falling upon her face or the cold wind swirling around her coat.

The ushers spread out the red carpet, unrolling it slowly from the door all the way down to the curb. They recognized Rosie. “Hi there,” said one of the ushers.

Rosie smiled bashfully. “Hello,” she answered.

A black limousine stopped at the curb, and an usher opened the door.

A girl about Rosie’s age jumped out, followed by a little boy. The girl’s blue wool coat was gathered at the waist and had covered buttons all the way to the top. She wore white gloves, white stockings, and shiny black shoes, the kind with a strap across the top. Her straight blond hair hung to her shoulders and at the back of her head was a pink bow. She grabbed her little brother by the hand and they ran into the theatre.

Then a tall slim lady emerged from the car. She was wearing an ankle-length black cape. She had black leather pointed shoes with very high heels. But as she stepped onto the red carpet, she slipped and almost fell into the snow. She caught herself though, and walked quickly into the theatre after the children. When she walked, the cape swirled and rustled in the wind.

For a moment, a cloud of sadness swept over Rosie. She put her hand in her pocket and stroked her little purse. So had Momma’s cape rustled in the wind.

More people arrived, all of them happy and excited to be at the theatre. Soon the ushers rolled up the carpet and closed the doors. It was time for Rosie to go home.

By now the snow was thick and heavy. Rosie put her head down into the wind. The street was empty.

Rosie couldn't see very clearly, and she slipped and fell flat on her back. She lay there while the snowflakes covered her face. She waved her hands up and down, making angel wings just as she used to do in Odessa.

Rosie's hand hit something in the snow. She dug down and pulled out a brown alligator leather wallet. She stood up, and looked around. The wooden doors were closed and the ushers were gone. There was no one to give the wallet to.

Rosie shoved it into her pocket. Bubba Sarah would know what to do.

Rosie hurried up the street to the streetcar. She sank into her seat, pulled off her sopping wet mitts and opened the wallet. She found a few dollars, and an identification card with an address and telephone number on it. Rosie stuck the wallet back in her pocket and watched the snow fall outside the windows of the streetcar.

Rosie ran through Mr. Yacobovitch's shop.

"Here, Rosie, some flowers. It's nice to see you smiling again." Mr. Yacobovitch handed Rosie the bouquet.

"Thanks Mr. Yacobovitch," she called as she ran up the stairs. "It's been a perfect Sunday, a really perfect day."

Rosie flew through the door.

"Bubba Sarah," she said. "Guess what? I saw this lady wearing a coat that swirled and rustled in the wind just like Momma's. And I saw a girl about my size. She had straight blond hair. I wish I had straight blond hair." Rosie jabbered on and on. "And, oh yes, I fell in the snow and found this wallet."

Bubba Sarah opened the wallet. There was the card with a name, and telephone number on it. "What does it say?" she asked.

"Mrs. Jo—hann—son, that's what it says," said Rosie, struggling with the letters.

"Go now, ask Mr. Yacobovitch if you can use his phone," said Bubba Sarah. "Call the lady. She will be worried."

"But Bubba Sarah, I think Mrs. Johannson might be one

of the ladies I saw outside the theatre. She's probably still at the ballet and she won't be home until later."

"Fine, we'll wait," said Bubba Sarah.

At six o'clock Rosie went downstairs. The telephone was on the wall inside Mr. Yacobovitch's shop. Rosie stood on her tiptoes and dialed the number carefully.

A woman answered the telephone.

"Hello," she said.

"Hello," Rosie said loudly. "Are you Mrs. Johannson? My name is Rosie. You don't know me but I was at the Royal Alexandra Theatre this afternoon and I found your wallet in the snow."

"Oh my goodness, I must have dropped it when I slipped getting out of the car," said Mrs. Johannson. "When may I come and pick it up?"

"Anytime," said Rosie. "I live with my grandmother at the corner of Dundas and Spadina Street. We live on top of Mr. Yacobovitch's flower shop. It's right where the streetcar stops. You can't miss it."

"Oh, I know that flower shop very well; I go there all the time," said Mrs. Johannson.

"You have to go through Mr. Yacobovitch's store to get to the stairs at the back," explained Rosie. "We're on the second floor. It's the green door at the end of the hall."

"The storm is getting worse," said Mrs. Johannson. "I'll be there as soon as I can. Thank you very much."

Chapter Twenty

Rosie climbed on top of the trunk and looked out the window. Soon a black limousine drove up. A tall slim lady stepped out. Rosie recognized the lady she had seen earlier. Behind her was the girl with straight blond hair still wearing her blue coat.

"Quick, Bubba Sarah," called Rosie. "She's here. Come see." Bubba Sarah looked out the window too.

A few minutes later there was a knock at the door. Rosie pulled at her yellow sweater and straightened her purple skirt. Bubba Sarah threw her apron over a chair and smoothed the kerchief over her hair. She opened the door. There stood Mrs. Johannson and the blond-haired girl Rosie had seen going into the theatre earlier that afternoon.

"*Gooten tag,* good day," said Bubba Sarah with a smile.

She held out her hand. "Please, you come in? Maybe a cup of tea?"

"This is my grandmother," said Rosie.

"How do you do," said Mrs. Johannson, shaking Bubba Sarah's hand. "Thank you for your offer of tea but we should return home quickly."

"This is my daughter Emily Anne," said Mrs. Johannson.

"Hi," said Emily Anne as she pushed a few strands of hair off her face. A silver barrette on one side kept it from falling in her eyes.

"Hi," said Rosie, twisting her braid. "Here's your wallet." She held the wallet out to Mrs. Johannson.

"Oh, thank you so very much," said Mrs. Johannson. "How lucky for me that you found it."

Emily Anne piped in. "Have you had that braid for a long time? I wish I had hair that long. My hair grows so slow. How old are you? I'm eleven, and I'll be twelve in four months."

"I'm eleven too, and I'll be twelve on January the seventh," said Rosie proudly.

Bubba Sarah and Mrs. Johannson smiled at each other.

Emily Anne hopped on one foot, and then the other. "Please Mommy," she said, tugging at her mother's coat, "can I ask her?"

"Yes, of course," said Mrs. Johannson.

"Mommy said that as a reward for finding her wallet, you're invited to come with us to the Swan Lake ballet. It's next Sunday at two o'clock at the Royal Alexandra Theatre. My little brother has a birthday party that day so we've got this extra ticket. Do you like ballet?" she asked, twisting her hair.

Rosie's eyes opened wide. "You really mean it?"

"Yes, of course we mean it," said Mrs. Johannson. "We would love you to come with us. We can pick you up. Your grandmother doesn't need to worry. We will take good care of you. I promise."

"Have you ever been to a ballet?" asked Emily Anne.

"Yes," said Rosie, lowering her eyes, "many times." She looked up at Bubba Sarah. "Can I go?"

"Well, maybe," said Bubba Sarah. She hesitated. She didn't know these people.

"Oh please, Bubba Sarah, please please," said Rosie.

"I understand how you feel," said Mrs. Johannson. "You can ask Mr. Yacobovitch about me. I am a good customer of his. Don't worry, Rosie will be safe with us."

"Okay," said Bubba Sarah. "It will be fine."

"Wonderful," said Mrs. Johannson. She smiled warmly at the two girls.

"I'm glad you can come with us," said Emily Anne.

"Thank you for inviting me," said Rosie.

"We must hurry now," said Mrs. Johannson. "The storm is getting worse. We'll be back to pick you up next Sunday at one o'clock. Is that all right?"

"I'll be ready," said Rosie.

"See you next Sunday," called Emily Anne as they hurried down the stairs. Bubba Sarah closed the door and turned to look at Rosie.

"I love you, Bubba Sarah," she shouted, jumping up and down. "I'm going to the ballet, me Rosie. I can't believe it. I'm really going to the ballet, and I'm going to wear my dream cape." She threw her cape over her shoulders, and grabbed Bubba Sarah. "Come, let's dance."

Bubba Sarah giggled. She held Rosie's hands, and she danced round and round the kitchen table, bobbing up and down, and then she sank into her chair to catch her breath.

Chapter Twenty-One

Rosie rushed to work extra early on Monday morning. She couldn't wait to talk to Gitel. There was so much she wanted to tell her.

"Rosie, you're back," said Gitel, surprised. "I missed you. I asked Yitzy where you were last week and he said you had business to do at home."

"I'll tell you everything at lunch," said Rosie.

Rosie opened her bench and took out her apron.

Fenya sauntered in late as usual. She took one look at Rosie. "Huh," she said, "what brings you back here? It was better around here without you. Nobody missed you, that's for sure." She poked Rosie in the back.

Rosie paid no attention to her. She was too happy to be

bothered by Fenya's teasing.

At lunch Rosie went to Yitzy's office and knocked on the door.

He opened the door. "And what can I do for you today?" he asked.

"I wanted to tell you my good news," said Rosie, her eyes sparkling with excitement. "I'm going to the ballet at the Royal Alexandra Theatre on Sunday and I'm going to wear my beautiful velvet cape. You see, I found a wallet in the snow at the theatre last Sunday and as a reward the lady offered to take me to the ballet."

"That's wonderful," said Yitzy. "I'm happy for you. You see it's good in Toronto," he said in a soft voice.

Gitel was right about Yitzy. Underneath that tough skin he was very gentle.

At lunch Rosie told Gitel everything. She told her about how she and Bubba Sarah had finished the cape, and how Bubba Sarah had surprised her by sewing the lining of the cape with the same material as Momma's, and about the sparkling button, and finding Mrs. Johannson's wallet and meeting Emily Anne, and best of all, the reward.

"Oh thank you, Gitel," said Rosie. "Thanks for talking to Yitzy and saving the scraps. I can't believe you did that for me."

"I wanted to help you," said Gitel, smiling shyly.

"Just think, Gitel, I'm going to the ballet on Sunday," said Rosie beaming with happiness. "Maybe someday, you and me, Gitel, we'll go to the ballet together. Wouldn't that be nice?"

"Sure would be, Rosie," said Gitel.

"But there's just one thing wrong."

"What's that?" asked Gitel.

"Well, you see, I had this empty baking soda can that had a painted girl on it, and I used it to store my own embroidery needles and scissors, and a special thimble that fit my finger, and they came from Odessa. But they're not in my bench. I've looked everywhere but I can't find my tin can and my sewing tools."

"That is strange," said Gitel, glancing over at Fenya's stool. She had a funny feeling about where Rosie's tin can might be. Fenya kept a green drawstring bag shoved in a corner on the floor beneath the ironing table. It was filled with lipstick and rouge, bottles of perfume samples, bobby pins, a hairbrush and an old address book.

While Fenya sat on the steps outside the factory eating her lunch, Gitel dumped the bag onto Rosie's table. There on the top of all the junk was Rosie's tin can with her sewing supplies.

Rosie jumped up and down and hugged Gitel. "Thank you, Gitel, thank you," said Rosie. "I sure am lucky to have you for a friend."

When Fenya came back, she noticed that her green bag had been moved. She shoved her hand into it and felt the bottom of the bag.

"Somebody's been fooling with my bag," she shouted. She stared at Rosie. "Who could it be? Come on, Gitel. Tell me, you know who it is."

Gitel just shrugged her shoulder. "Who cares about your bag?"

"Well, I'll bet I know who touched my bag," said Fenya. "Listen here, Miss Rosie, you wanna take my advice if you don't want to go back to where you came from, from now on stay out of my things. Got it?" She shoved the bag into her coat pocket. "Can't leave anything around here anymore," she said shaking her head.

Rosie looked over to Gitel and gave her a small smile. Gitel was sitting up straight and she smiled back. The factory no longer seemed so unfriendly.

Chapter Twenty-Two

Sunday finally came.

"Today, Rosie," said Bubba Sarah, "there are no chores for you. They can wait. Come sit on the stool. I will do your hair."

Rosie climbed on top of the wooden stool next to the full-length mirror. Rosie twisted and turned, picturing how she would look in her dream cape.

Bubba Sarah opened a jar of gel.

"Where did you get the gel, Bubba Sarah?" asked Rosie.

"Mrs. Sobcuff brought it to me. When I told her I was going to fix your hair in ringlets, she offered to bring it."

Rosie clapped her hands excitedly.

"Sit still," said Bubba Sarah, "if you want me to make those curls, ringlets, you must sit still."

Today wasn't the best day for Rosie to sit still.

Bubba Sarah took a thin lock of Rosie's hair in one hand, brushed some gel on it and then rolled the hair around the finger of her other hand. And when there was no hair left to roll, she gently let the curl drop. "A nice ringlet," she said. Then she made another, and another, all over Rosie's head.

Rosie got down from the stool and stood in front of the long mirror. She moved her head from side to side. The curls all stayed in place.

"Oh Bubba Sarah," she said. "It's exactly the way Momma used to do it."

"So, who do you think taught your Momma?" Bubba Sarah chuckled.

A few minutes before one o'clock, Bubba Sarah gently draped the cape over Rosie's shoulders. She smoothed out the velvet, and fixed the hood so Rosie's ringlets could be seen, and she pushed the sparkling button through the hole at her neck.

"Like a queen, you look," she said. "It's a wonderful cape, Rosie."

Rosie took her little red and black flowered change purse from under her pillow, counted the eighteen pennies inside, and dropped it into the pocket of the cape. She climbed on top of the trunk and watched the street outside the window.

At exactly one o'clock the big black car stopped in front of Mr. Yacobovitch's shop.

"You're beautiful today"

"They're here, Bubba Sarah, they're here."

Bubba Sarah kissed Rosie on the forehead. "You see my child, even in Toronto, dreams can come true."

Rosie walked down the stairs very slowly, lifting the cape so it wouldn't drag on the dirty steps.

Mr. Yacobovitch was waiting for her. "You're beautiful today," he said. And he handed her three red roses, each separately wrapped in pink paper and tied with a red ribbon that curled at the ends.

"A little something for you and your friends," he said proudly.

Bubba Sarah had told Mr. Yacobovitch everything.

"Thank you, Mr. Yacobovitch," said Rosie. "They are lovely."

Rosie walked outside to the car, where Emily Anne and her mother were waiting. She turned to look up at the apartment window. Bubba Sarah was waving at her. She had a big smile and tears of joy rolling down her cheeks. Rosie waved back and waited as the driver opened the door. She lifted her cape and climbed into the big black car.

Chapter Twenty-Three

"Hi Rosie," said Emily Anne. "Sit in the middle, between me and Mommy."

"Hello," said Rosie smiling. She sat between the two of them and then handed Mrs. Johannson and Emily Anne each a rose.

"From Mr. Yacobovitch," she said.

"How thoughtful of Mr. Yacobovitch," said Mrs. Johannson.

Rosie pulled her cape from under her and smoothed it upon the seat so it wouldn't get crushed.

"Oh Rosie, you're as pretty as a princess," said Emily Anne. "I love your curls. And your cape, it's the most beautiful cape I've ever seen." She rubbed her hand over the red patches. "Mommy can you buy me one just like this, please can you?"

"If Rosie doesn't mind you having the same cape as hers," said Mrs. Johannson.

"Where did you buy it? Would you mind if I got the same colour?" asked Emily Anne.

"I didn't buy it," said Rosie. "I . . . I made it."

"You mean you sewed it yourself?" asked Emily Anne. She and her mother looked very surprised. "How? Where did you get the material?"

"From the factory, where I work," said Rosie, looking down at her hands.

"How did you come to work at the factory, Rosie?" asked Mrs. Johannson in a warm and understanding voice.

Rosie told them about her old life in Odessa and her new life in Toronto. She told them how the Cossacks had taken away Momma, a ballerina, and how Bubba Sarah and she had fled to Canada. She told them about working in the factory and about the scraps, and how her friend Gitel and Yitzy the factory boss had helped her. And she told them about the lining that Bubba Sarah saved, and Momma's sparkling button. Finally Rosie told them how every Sunday she went to the Royal Alexandra Theatre and how she dreamed that maybe one day she would go to the ballet just as she used to in Russia.

"Now I understand," said Mrs. Johannson. "That's how

you found my wallet last Sunday." Her voice was soft and friendly. Rosie was glad that she had shared her story with Emily Anne and her mother.

"Rosie, we're here!" Emily Anne clapped her hands excitedly. The black limousine drove up to the curb and parked right in front of the Royal Alexandra Theatre.

An usher stepped up to the car and opened the door. Rosie and Emily Anne jumped out and hurried down the red carpet. Mrs. Johannson followed behind them.

Rosie looked up at the big roof with its row of sparkling lights. This time she would be going inside the theatre instead of watching everyone else go inside. A second usher held the wooden carved doors open. Rosie smiled at him and he smiled back in recognition.

"Very pretty," he said with a big smile.

Rosie blushed. "Thank you," she said shyly.

Hand-in-hand, Rosie and Emily Anne walked into the lobby. The lights in the chandelier made the crystals glitter like stars.

Mrs. Johannson handed the tickets to the usher. "Go upstairs to the balcony. The first row in the center," he said.

They climbed the circular staircase up to the balcony.

Mrs. Johannson knew where their seats were.

They sat in the first row, right in the center.

"I hope you like these seats," said Emily Anne. "Mommy says they're the best seats because the balcony in this theatre is close to the stage, and we get to see the dancers' faces better."

"Yes," said Rosie, "they're perfect seats." She smiled at Mrs. Johannson.

Emily Anne linked her arm in Rosie's. "Maybe someday, Rosie," she said, "you can teach me how to sew a velvet cape."

"Maybe," said Rosie with a twinkle in her eye. "Maybe someday."

The lights dimmed and suddenly the orchestra burst into music. The red and orange silk curtain shimmered as it slowly lifted to the ceiling.

And the dancers floated onto the stage, one by one, on tiptoes.

A tear rolled down Rosie's cheek. Here am I, Rosie, in Toronto, Canada, wearing my dream cape to the ballet. If only Momma could be here now.

Rosie slipped her hand into her pocket. She gently picked up the red and black flowered change purse, and squeezed her fingers over the soft fabric.

Yes, she was the luckiest girl in the world.

WONDER WHAT HAPPENED TO ROSIE?

While working in Yitzy's factory, Rosie heard the girls (women were often called "girls" in those days) talking about a horrible fire at the Triangle Shirtwaist Company factory in New York City on March 25, 1911. At that factory there were no fire extinguishers, no fire escapes and a single door leading to a narrow wooden staircase. The fire ladders reached only to the 3rd floor. The factory was on the 5th, 6th, and 7th floors of a tall brick building. One hundred and forty-six girls died. Soon after this fire, the workers in New York joined together to start unions and clubs. Their purpose was to make the factories safer by providing fire escapes, more exits, proper lunch rooms and bathrooms, and whatever else the girls needed for a safe working environment.

With Gitel's assistance, Rosie organized the first union in Yitzy's factory. The girls met every month to talk about ways to make the building safer. And every month they paid money or "dues" to the union. Rosie said it was important that they have extra money in the bank in case something happened, or someone needed help. Yitzy fought the idea of workers' safety for several years, but after the union was formed he listened to Rosie's requests. She told Yitzy that the girls wouldn't come to work if he didn't fix the broken windows, exposed electrical wiring and other dangerous things in his factory. They said they wouldn't work, not just for a day, but for a very long time. They would go on strike. Naturally Yitzy was not too happy about this, since he had orders to fill and he thought the improvements would be too costly. The girls worked hard to convince Yitzy of the benefits of employee safety and better working conditions. Finally Yitzy agreed. He fixed the broken window, put in brighter lights, replaced the wiring and repaired the toilet. In addition, the girls did not have to work on weekends anymore and had Christmas Day and Easter Monday off. Yitzy paid them two dollars more a month and, for the first time, the girls could speak up or make a complaint without worrying about being fired.

Rosie continued to work at Yitzy's factory, eventually becoming a manager. When she was nineteen, she left to be married. All her life Rosie remained proud of her role in organizing the union and helping the other workers to a better life.

Bubba Sarah died when Rosie was seventeen. But before her death, she arranged with Mr. Yacobovitch for Rosie to remain in the apartment. Rosie paid as much rent as she could, and every weekend she worked in Mr. Yacobovitch's store. He had promised Bubba Sarah that he would look out for Rosie, and he did, until she left to start a new home with her husband. Rosie kept in touch with Mr. Yacobovitch for many years after.

In her new home, Rosie ordered patterns from the *Woman's Home Companion* magazine, and she sewed all her own clothes. She never stopped sewing. At home, she sewed aprons, tablecloths, curtains, oven mitts and place mats, and sold them all at the Kensington market.

Occasionally Rosie bumped into Fenya on the street but they never became friends. Gitel and Rosie, however, maintained a lifelong friendship.

Every Christmas and Easter for the next few years, Rosie received a card from Mrs. Johannson and Emily Anne, and about twice a year they talked on the telephone. In spite of her good intentions, Emily Anne never took sewing lessons from Rosie.

Rosie always saved as much money as possible, but whenever she had a little extra, she would buy a cheap "standing room only" ticket to the Royal Alexandra Theatre for the ballet.

As for me, the author, I still have my Momma Rosie's tin can filled with her buttons and needles and thimble. But best of all, I carry around in my purse, for good luck, the little red and black flowered change purse. You know, the one with the eighteen pennies in it.

Zelda Freedman

ABOUT THE AUTHOR

Zelda Freedman is a retired medical librarian with a diploma in Library Science from Algonquin College, Ottawa. As department head, she was responsible for establishing the medical library at Elisabeth Bruyere Health Center, Ottawa, a 300-bed long-term, chronic and palliative care facility. She is a graduate of the Institute of Children's Literature, Redding, Connecticut, and a member of the Society of Children's Book Writers and Illustrators. A professional writer for the last eleven years, she is the author of the book *Pleased To See You: You Have a Right To Ask.* In fulfilment of a promise to her mother, she wrote *Rosie's Dream Cape,* her first novel for children. Since her retirement in 1991, she has become a professional painter, a potter and a weaver, with a number of juried exhibitions. Zelda Freedman is the mother of four, and the grandmother of one. She lives in Ottawa, Ontario.